For Sale:
One Sister – Cheap!

Written by Katie Alder and
Rachael McBride

Illustrated by Mike Venezia

CHILDRENS PRESS ®
CHICAGO

To Louis and Sue Alder and David and Linda McBride

Library of Congress Cataloging-in-Publication Data

Alder, Katie.
　For sale, one sister cheap.

　Summary: Sarah makes such a pest of herself that her
big brother decides to get rid of her by selling her.
　[1.　Brothers and sisters—Fiction]　I.　McBride,
Rachael.　II.　Title.
PZ7.A361F0　1986　　　[E]　　　86-11723
ISBN 0-516-03476-6

My little sister, Sarah, made me so mad one day, I decided to sell her. If that sounds mean, wait until I tell you what she did.

I was finger painting yesterday and Sarah took a tube of toothpaste and squirted all over my painting!

Mom said she was just trying to help.
But I think she did it on purpose.
That's not all she did.

At lunch she poured her green pea
soup all over my baloney sandwich.
Mom said it was an accident.
But I think she did it on purpose.
That was bad enough. But that's not
all she did.

Last night she tore up my homework for the bottom of her hamster cage.

Mom said Sarah thought it was scrap paper.

But I think she did it on purpose.

So early this morning, Mom went to get money to pay the milkman.

I thought it would be better to trade my sister. It would have saved a lot of money.

But the milkman said he already had a little girl.

Then I took Sarah to Joey's house to see if he would buy her. Joey always wanted a little sister.

I told him I'd trade her for two of his new trucks. When he said, "No deal," I told him I'd trade her for two of his old trucks.

He still said no.

I guess he didn't really want a little sister.

Some of my friends had a lemonade stand. They offered to help me sell Sarah. They were glad to help, because they think little sisters are a pain in the neck, too.

We almost sold her to one girl who wanted a friend.

But she decided she'd rather have one more glass of lemonade.

I thought someone at the grocery store might want to buy Sarah. So I taped a "For Sale" sign on her back and pulled her in my little orange wagon with green racing stripes.

She thought I was just taking her for a ride.

15

A skinny girl with red hair and freckles was going to give me a candy bar for her.

But at the last minute she
changed her mind.
I didn't like that kind of candy
bar anyway.

A policeman came by and asked
where we were going.
I told him I was selling Sarah.

He bought her for three cents.
At last I got rid of her.

On the way home the wagon was easy
to pull. But there was no one to talk to.

20

At the lemonade stand there was a
little girl that sort of looked like Sarah.
I offered her a ride in my wagon. But
she said she didn't like boys.

Sarah likes boys.

Playing with Joey wasn't much fun either, without Sarah. He was mean. Joey likes little sisters.

I didn't want to go home. Mom would make me eat all the green pea soup!

Sarah likes green pea soup.

But as soon as I opened the door, my sister ran up and hugged me.
I was so surprised that the policeman had brought her home that I hugged her back.

I didn't mean to hug her.
Hugs are for sissies. But. . .

. . . Sarah said I did it on purpose.

About the Authors

Katie Alder has been a little sister for twenty one years. Her brother has never tried to sell her. . .yet, but he is an accomplished little-sister-teaser. He gave her one nickname which still sticks—"Brutus." Katie was born and raised in Virginia and has lived in Ohio and England. She currently lives in California. She is majoring in English and Education at Brigham Young University in Provo, Utah.

One of ten children, Rachael McBride was born in Pasadena, California. When she was two, the McBride family moved to Corona, California. She was a Child Psychology major at Utah Technical College in Orem, Utah when she and Katie Alder wrote *For Sale—One Sister Cheap*. Rachael is currently attending Brigham Young University in Hawaii and working as a preschool teacher at a Child-Parent Center.

About the Artist

Mike Venezia is a graduate of the School of the Art Institute of Chicago. When not working on children's books, Mike is a busy art director for a large midwestern advertising company. He is also the father of Michael Anthony and Elizabeth Ann. This is the ninth book he has illustrated for Childrens Press.